DATE DUE			
MAY 24			
JUN 07			

4 / 00

JACKSON COUNTY
Library Services

HEADQUARTERS
413 West Main Street
Medford, Oregon 97501

To my dad, S.M. Brozovich, who taught me to fish. —KLF

For Tara — Fish on! —BL

Text © 1999 by Kristine L. Franklin.
Illustrations © 1999 by Barbara Lavallee.

Book and jacket design by Kristine Brogno and Juliana Van Horn.
Typeset in Nofret.
Printed in Hong Kong.

Library of Congress Information
Franklin, Kristine L.
The gift / by Kristine L. Franklin; illustrated by Barbara Lavallee.
p. cm.
Summary: Although some in town consider the Fish Woman a witch, a
young boy goes fishing with her and not only catches, and gives away, his
first salmon, but gets to see a pod of whales close up.
ISBN 0-8118-0447-x
[1. Fishing–Fiction. 2. Whales–Fiction. 3. Old age–Fiction.]
I. Lavallee, Barbara, ill. II. Title
PZ7.F859226G1   1999
[E] -- dc21   97-24561
                  CIP
                  AC

Distributed in Canada by Raincoast Books
8680 Cambie Street
Vancouver B.C. V6P 6M9

10 9 8 7 6 5 4 3 2 1

Chronicle Books
85 Second Street
San Francisco, California 94105

www.chroniclebooks.com/Kids

The Gift

by KRISTINE L. FRANKLIN

illustrated by BARBARA LAVALLEE

chronicle books · san francisco

In a place by the sea, where the winters are wet and the summers are cool and tall trees stand guard like soldiers along the shoreline, there lived a boy named Jimmy Joe. When he wasn't in school, Jimmy Joe liked to throw sticks to his dog, climb trees and chase seagulls. But like his father and his grandfather and all the fathers before him, more than anything else, Jimmy Joe loved to fish.

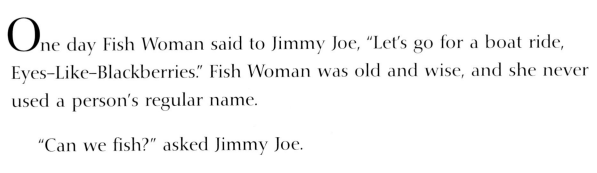

One day Fish Woman said to Jimmy Joe, "Let's go for a boat ride, Eyes-Like-Blackberries." Fish Woman was old and wise, and she never used a person's regular name.

"Can we fish?" asked Jimmy Joe.

"Of course," said Fish Woman. "Why else would we go?"

Jimmy Joe ran home to ask his mother.

"Fish Woman knows everything about the sea, doesn't she?" asked Jimmy Joe. His mother nodded and tugged a sweater over his head.

"She knows the weather and the tides and where to fish and what to take for bait, right?" Jimmy Joe's mother nodded again and pulled a wool hat down over his ears.

Some people said that Fish Woman was a sea witch, and that her spit could kill a dogfish. "She's not really a witch, is she?" Jimmy Joe asked his mother.

Jimmy Joe's mother smiled, but "Catch a few dozen," was all she said.

Jimmy Joe promised his mother a bucketful of fish and hurried down to the beach.

Fish Woman lived in a tumbled–down shack right on the beach. Once it had been white. Now it was the soft color of a rain cloud. In front of the house, just below the timber bulkhead, Fish Woman was pouring gasoline into an out-board motor. The sharp smell of the gasoline mixed with the salty sea. It was a good smell, a fishing smell.

"Climb aboard," shouted Fish Woman. Jimmy Joe took his seat in the bow, then Fish Woman heaved the little boat into deep water and hopped aboard as nimbly as a squirrel.

The outboard motor started with a roar.

"What are we after?" shouted Jimmy Joe.

"What are you after?" Fish Woman shouted back.

Jimmy Joe thought of the cod and sole and sea perch he would bring to his mother. "Stew fish," he yelled.

"I know something better than stew fish," Fish Woman hollered above the sound of the motor.

"Salmon?" asked Jimmy Joe. Fish Woman headed the boat toward Chinook Point.

"I'm going to catch a big salmon!" yelled Jimmy Joe.

"I know something even better than salmon," shouted Fish Woman. She grinned until her eyes nearly disappeared.

Jimmy Joe peeked over the side of the boat into the green water to see if the salmon were running. Fish Woman laughed. "Do you think they swim up here where you can see them?" Jimmy Joe smiled and shook his head. He didn't know what salmon did when they were running. He only wanted to catch one and take it home.

When they got to Chinook Point, Fish Woman cut the motor. Jimmy Joe dropped the anchor overboard. He was careful not to let the nylon rope burn his hands as it whizzed into the deep. The water made a thick, salty plop as Jimmy Joe's bait and weights disappeared into the bay.

"If you hook a salmon," said Fish Woman as she tossed her rig into the water, "let me know. You'll need help."

Jimmy Joe was sure he wouldn't need any help.

For a long time, nothing happened.
The fish weren't biting, not even a
nibble. The water was flat and slick
and gray. Jimmy Joe grew tired
of sitting.

A big fish hit just as the wet fog rolled in. Jimmy Joe knocked over the bait bucket with his foot. The herring flipped about in the bottom of the boat. The water soaked Jimmy Joe's shoes. Suddenly Jimmy Joe was slipping, falling.

Fish Woman grabbed him around the middle. One bony fist clamped around the fishing rod. "It's a salmon, Eyes–Like–Blackberries," she whispered. "Keep your rod in the air." Jimmy Joe's heart flipped and flopped like the big fish.

"Hang on," yelled Fish Woman. "He'll try to run under the boat – keep the tip up!" Jimmy Joe cranked and slackened and pulled. Together they held on tight. His arms and back began to ache, but he didn't let go. Finally they brought the tired salmon to the boat. It was enormous.

Jimmy Joe helped Fish Woman lift the salmon onto some crushed ice. The fish was bigger than he could reach with both arms spread wide. Its skin glittered silver and gold, like a pirate's treasure. None of Jimmy Joe's friends had ever caught a Chinook. It was something to be proud of. But something was wrong.

Jimmy Joe tried to feel happy. He imagined the surprise on his mother's face when he brought home such a huge fish. But looking at the beautiful, dead fish made Jimmy Joe feel cold inside.

Then, through the thickening fog, Jimmy Joe heard a strange sound. *Pfffffsst-HAH!* It was a long way off. *Pfffffsst-HAH! Pfffffsst-HAH!* But soon the sound got louder and louder, closer and closer. *Pfffffsst-HAH!*

All at once Jimmy Joe saw nine glossy black backs and sharp dorsal fins in the water. *Pfffffsst-HAH!* went the sound, exhaled through blowholes the size of his fist.

And then he heard Fish Woman whisper a single word: "Welcome."

One whale moved in close. The fin on its back stood as tall as Jimmy Joe. Jimmy Joe shivered. His heart rattled and thumped, but he wanted to see the whale. He inched toward the edge of the boat. Beside him in the water was the largest animal he had ever seen.

"What do they want?" asked Jimmy Joe in a voice that quivered like a jellyfish.

"They want the same thing you do. Food." Jimmy Joe's eyes opened wide.
Fish Woman grinned. "Salmon, boy. They're hunting salmon. The Wolves of
the Sea don't waste their time on skinny boys and tough old women."

As if it had heard her words, the whale rolled playfully to one side. Jimmy
Joe saw its bright, white underbelly and its huge mouth curled up in a
permanent smile. It was almost close enough to touch.

The whale looked carefully at Jimmy Joe's face. It waved one flipper in the air and then *SPLASH*, smacked it down hard on the water.

Pfffffsst-HAH! The whale blew a spray of fishy breath in Jimmy Joe's face. Then, the whale rolled over and looked Jimmy Joe straight in the eye. This time its grin was for Jimmy Joe.

Fish Woman laughed out loud. The sudden noise startled the whale. It slipped below the surface and moved away. "Come back!" called Jimmy Joe. But the whale had disappeared.

Jimmy Joe looked at Fish Woman. Then he looked at the salmon.

Jimmy Joe tried to lift the salmon by himself, but it was heavy and slick. Fish Woman helped him. Together they slipped the big fish into the sea.

Suddenly the whale sped back toward the boat. With one monstrous gulp, it grabbed the fish and dove out of sight. The little boat danced and jumped in its wake. Jimmy Joe heard *Pfffffsst-HAH!* in the distance, but he couldn't see through the fog. He looked for the other whales, but they were gone.

"Bring them back!" cried Jimmy Joe, looking at Fish Woman.

"Me?" asked Fish Woman with a surprised look. She shook her head. "When the great Wolves of the Sea choose to show themselves, it is a gift."

"It's better than cod or sole or sea perch," whispered Jimmy Joe. "It's better than catching a salmon."

"I'm glad you think so, Eyes–Like–Blackberries," said Fish Woman. She patted Jimmy Joe's hand and grinned so hard her eyes disappeared. "And now," she said, "let's go catch that bucket of stew fish."